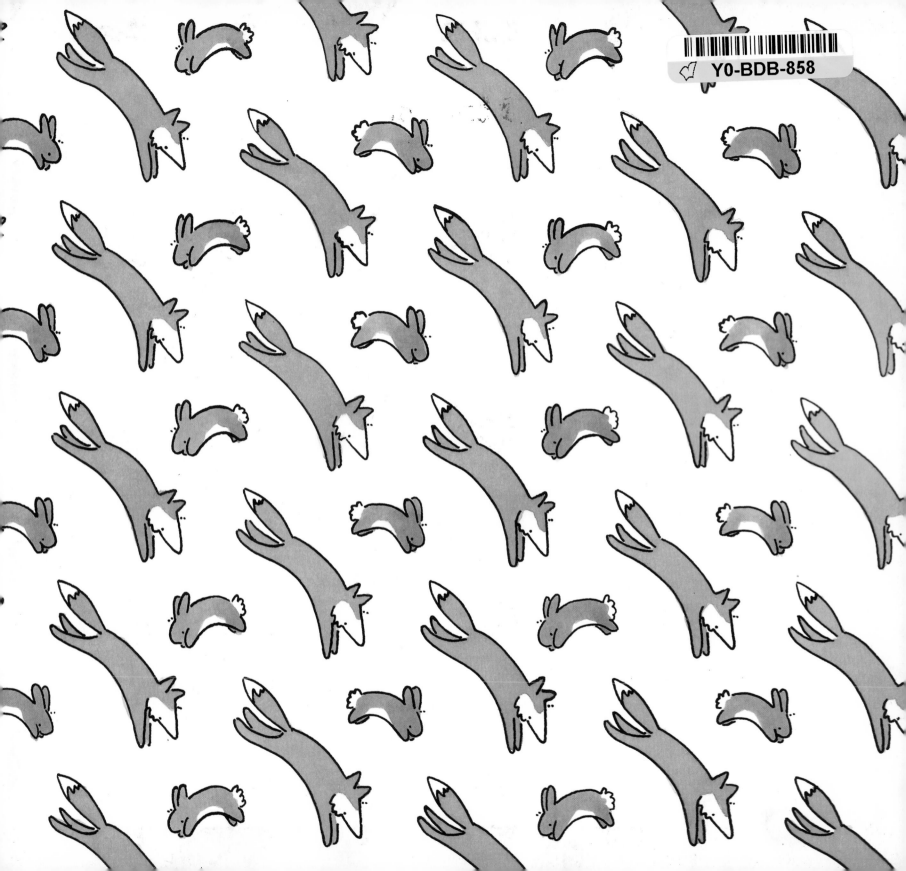

For Andi

Published by Ideals Children's Books
an imprint of Hambleton-Hill Publishing, Inc.
Nashville, Tennessee 37218

Printed and bound in Belgium.

ISBN 0-8249-8649-0

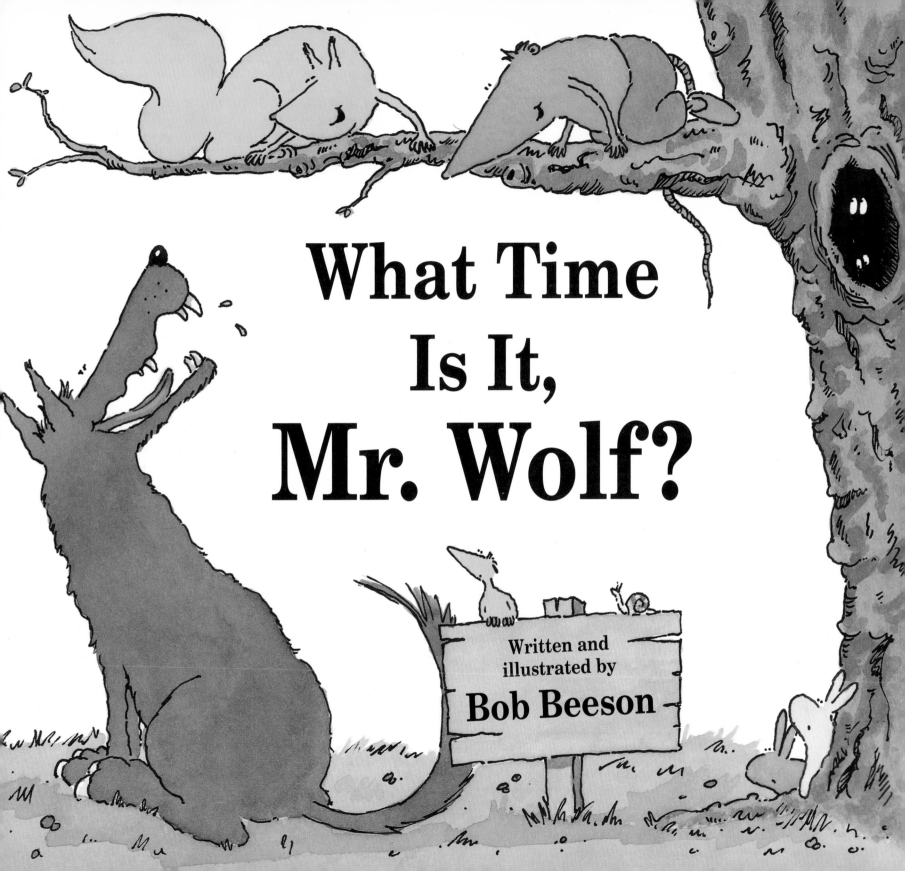

What Time Is It, Mr. Wolf?

Written and illustrated by

Bob Beeson

What time is it, Mr. Wolf?
8 o'clock and time to get up.

Oops, I'm sorry, Mr. Wolf.

What time is it, Mr. Wolf?
9 o'clock and time for a wolf-sized breakfast.

That will teach you to be greedy, Mr. Wolf.

What time is it, Mr. Wolf?
10 o'clock and time to play outside.

Oh, bad luck, Mr. Wolf.

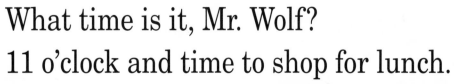 What time is it, Mr. Wolf?
11 o'clock and time to shop for lunch.

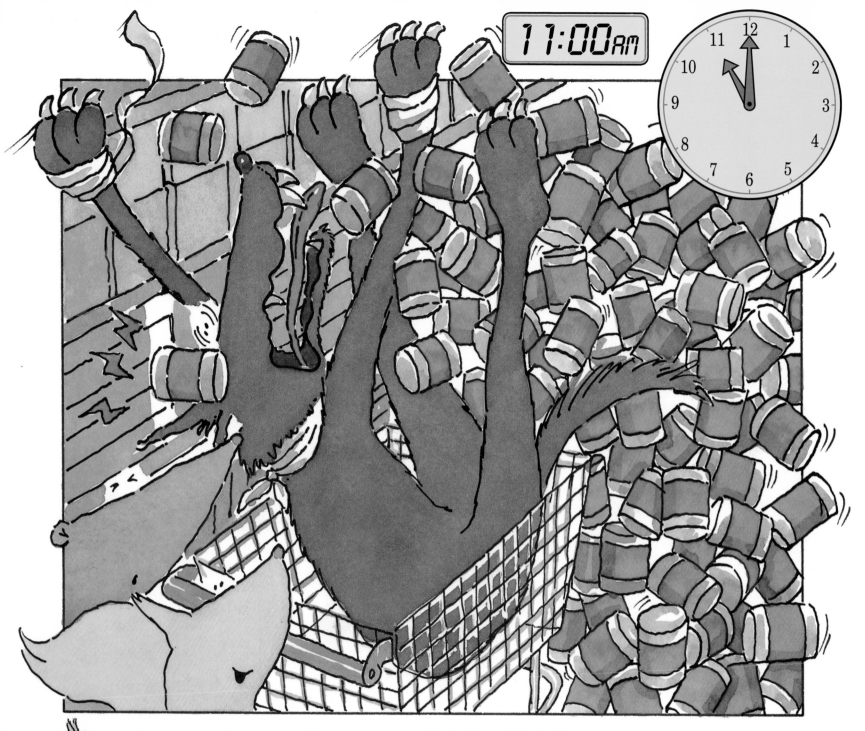

Do you have all you need, Mr. Wolf?

What time is it, Mr. Wolf?

12 o'clock and lunchtime for a hungry wolf.

Ouch! I'll bet that hurt, Mr. Wolf!

 What time is it, Mr. Wolf?
1 o'clock and time to play.

So sorry, Mr. Wolf.

What time is it, Mr. Wolf?
2 o'clock and time for a quick swim.

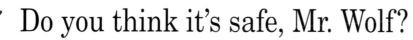 Do you think it's safe, Mr. Wolf?

 What time is it, Mr. Wolf?

3 o'clock and time for a wolf-sized snack.

I'll bet that smarts, Mr. Wolf.

What time is it now, Mr. Wolf?
4 o'clock and time to clean up.

Watch your step, Mr. Wolf!

 What time is it, Mr. Wolf?
5 o'clock and time to wash up for dinner.

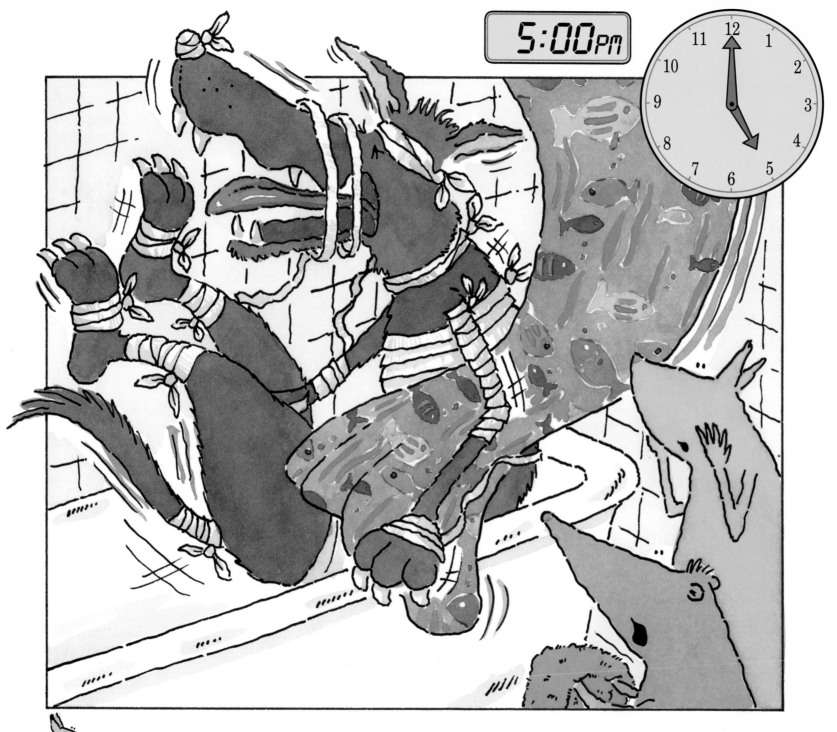

Careful, Mr. Wolf! Baths can be slippery places.

What time is it, Mr. Wolf?
6 o'clock and time for a hungry wolf's dinner.

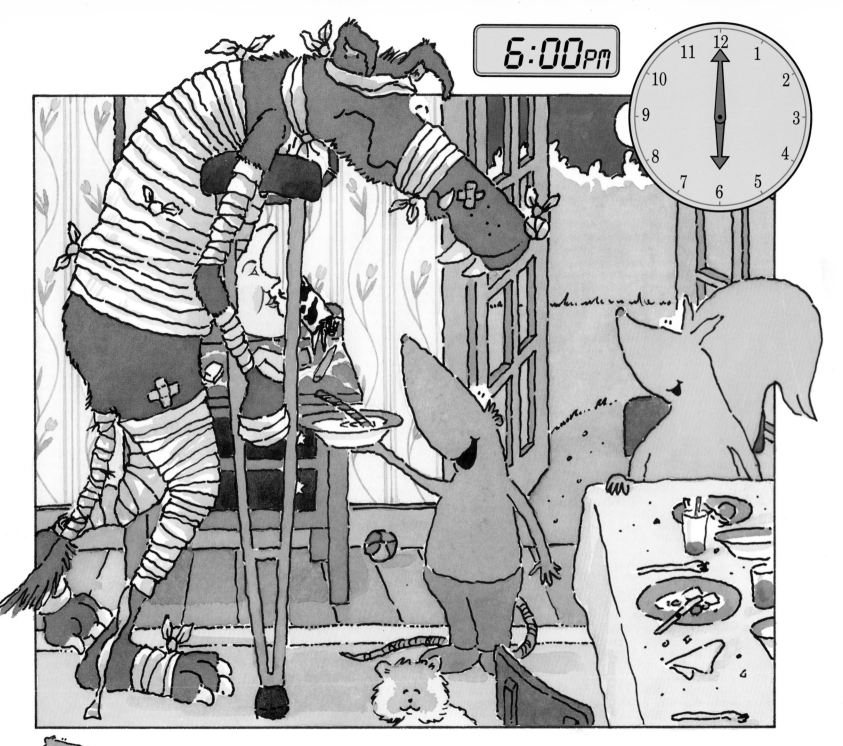

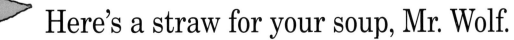 Here's a straw for your soup, Mr. Wolf.

 What time is it, Mr. Wolf?
7 o'clock and time for bed.

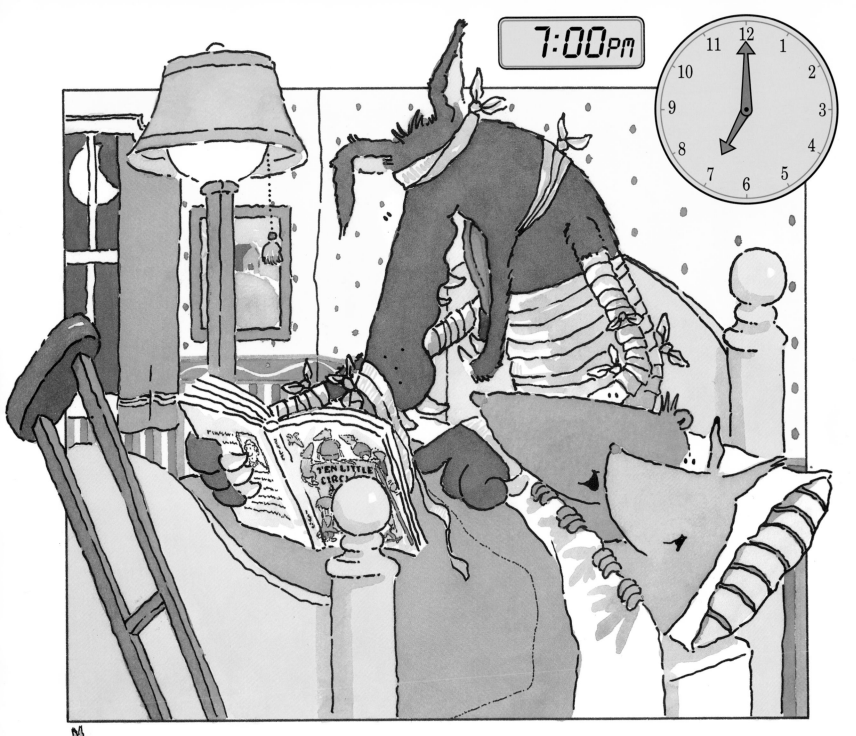

Great story, Mr. Wolf!

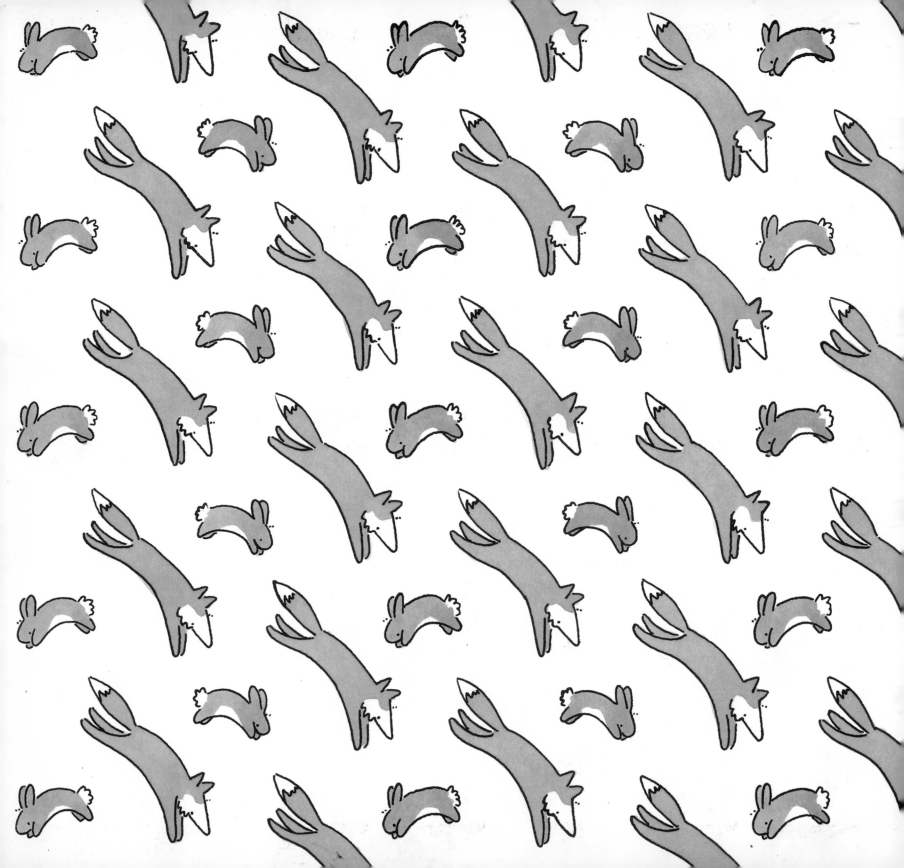